D0130013

Please return on or before the latest date above.
You can renew online at www.kent.gov.uk/libs
or by phone 08458 247 200

CARTER S

CUSTOMER SERVICE EXCELLENCE

Libraries & Archives

Kent
County
Council

C153817722

*Thanks to Mom and Dad for their love and for letting me
have lots of pets when I was little! – TF*

First published in 2009
by Franklin Watts

Text © Deborah Smith and Tina Freeth 2009
Illustrations © Dan Chernett 2009
Cover design by Peter Scoulding

Franklin Watts
338 Euston Road
London NW1 3BH

Franklin Watts Australia
Level 17/207 Kent Street
Sydney, NSW 2000

A CIP catalogue record for this book
is available from the British Library.

ISBN: 978 0 7496 9039 7

1 3 5 7 9 10 8 6 4 2

Printed in Great Britain by J F Print Ltd., Sparkford, Somerset

Franklin Watts is a division of Hachette Children's Books,
an Hachette UK company.
www.hachette.co.uk

Harvey, Sam, Amber, Ravi, Jade and Lewis are:

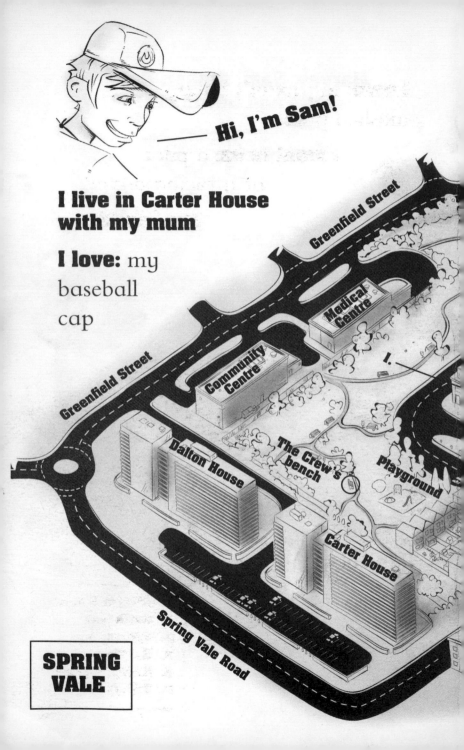

I hate: my mum's lumpy mashed potato

I want to be: a pilot or a racing driver

Best word: *fast*

1. Chicken House
2. Sleek Lady
3. Sun and Sea
4. Hot Wok
5. Empty shop unit
6. 8 To Late

Chapter One

"Sam, will ya watch Buster for me?"
Calvin asks.

"For sure!" I tell him.

Buster is a massive dog.

Calvin is massive too.

"I'll give ya ten pounds for it,"
Calvin says.

"Great!" I say.

"Don't lose him," Calvin warns me.

"I won't," I tell Calvin.

"Better not – or else," he says.

Then he hands me Buster's lead.

I look well hard with Buster, but he is strong.

He is yanking my arm out!

I walk to the playground to meet the Crew.

"Hey! Look what I got!" I say.

"That dog is BIG, man!" says Harvey.

"He's Calvin's — his name is Buster," I tell them.

"Yeah, they look like each other, innit!" Ravi says.

"Does he bite?" Jade asks.

"Nah!" I say.

"Come on, let's walk him," says Amber.

We walk out of the park, past a Cheetas car.

The Cheetas are an older crew.

Buster stops and sniffs a tyre.

He lifts his leg.

"No, Buster!" I hiss.

He wags his tail at me.

Then he wets all over the back wheel.

"Let's get out of here!" I say.

We hurry off down the road.

"Who wants some food?" Harvey asks.

"Me!" says Ravi.

"Me too!" says Amber.

"Me three!" says Jade with a grin.

I join in the joke. "Me four!" I add.

Then Lewis yells, "Me too!"

We all roll our eyes.

"Lewis, you fool! You gotta say – me five!" I tell him.

Lewis shakes his head.

He never gets it.

"I've got no cash," I say.

"No sweat, Sam – we'll pay for you," says Amber.

Ravi nods. "We can get loads of stuff and share it out."

"Cool, let's do it," says Harvey.

We walk across the playing field.

The 8 To Late is on the other side.

"Eeeuww! NASTY! Look at that man over there," says Jade.

We all look.

A man is putting his dog's poo in a plastic bag.

"EEEUWW!" the others all shout.

"Sam, you're gonna have to pick up Buster's poo!" Lewis grins.

"You joker – I don't think so!" I tell him.

I really hope Buster won't poo.

Not until he is back with Calvin.

We get to the 8 To Late.

Jade points to the door. A sign says 'NO DOGS'.

"I'll stay out here with Buster then," I tell the others.

They nod and go into the shop.

"Won't be long, Sam!" Ravi calls.

Chapter Two

Some hot girls come out of the Chicken House.

Cool. Girls like dogs.

I smile at them, but they just smile at Buster. Then Buster sees a cat.

He gives a MASSIVE yank on the lead.

I can't hold him back!

"BUSTER! NO!" I yell.

He drags me along with him and I trip over.

Buster's lead slips out of my hand.

I hit the ground. "OWWWWW!"

He runs off, after the cat.

"Buster! Come back!" I yell.

I can't lose Buster. Calvin will kill me – big time!

The stupid girls just stand there laughing.

Buster follows the cat around the corner. Oh, no!

I'm in BIG trouble now...

Then the door to Sleek Lady shoots open.

A man runs out.

"Stop that robber!" a woman screams from inside the shop.

It's Carla – who owns Sleek Lady.

The robber falls over me!

"What the…ARGGHH!" he yells.

"OWWWWW!" I yell back.

Carla runs out then.

A big woman with half a haircut follows her.

"Hah!" they shout, seeing the robber on the ground.

Carla grabs back her cash.

"I'm going to call the police," she tells the woman.

"Don't let him get away!"

She runs back inside.

"OOOFF!" goes the robber.

The woman has sat on him –
and me!

"Ouch!" I squeak.

"Get off!" the robber yells.

"No, I will not!" the woman
yells back. "This is what you get
for robbing!" she says.

How did I get into this?

People come out to see what's going on.

I sure hope the Crew come soon!

"So where is Sam?"

That's Jade's voice.

At last!

"Guys! Guys! I'm under here!" I yell.

The Crew hear me and come rushing over.

The woman hears me too.

She looks down with a frown.

"Eh? What are you doing down there?" she growls.

"Sorry. I got in the way," I tell her.

"You silly boy!" she says.

"Can I get up now?" I ask.

The woman tuts loudly. Then she stands up.

"Move over!" she snaps at the robber.

The robber rolls off me. I'm free!

The robber makes a run for it!

The woman grabs his hood.

She pulls him back.

"Don't even think about it!" she growls.

She pushes the robber back down and sits on him again.

"Better not mess with her, bro!" Harvey says.

Carla comes out of Sleek Lady.

"I can finish your cut while we wait for the police," she tells the woman.

"Great!" the woman says. "Don't wanna waste time on this robber!" she adds.

Then she gives the robber a poke in the ribs.

"Owww!" he yells.

We all watch as Carla cuts the woman's hair.

Chapter Three

"So how did all this happen?" Amber asks.

"Well, first of all, Buster pulls me over…" I tell them.

Then my mouth falls open.

"BUSTER!" we all say.

In all the fuss, we forgot Buster!

"He ran off after a cat," I go on.

I feel sick.

I've lost Buster.

I am in soooo much trouble.

"Oh! Poor Buster!" Amber says.
"He's lost!"

"Poor Buster? Poor me!" I tell her.
"Calvin is gonna kill me!"

"Don't worry, Sam. We'll help you
find him," says Jade.

"Where shall we look first?" Lewis asks.

I point the way Buster ran off.

"He ran round the corner," I say.

"Come on, let's go!" says Harvey.

We call out, "Buster! Here, boy!" as we walk.

We cross Lark Street, past the school.

But there is no Buster.

A woman comes along with her dog.

"Have you seen a dog running after a cat?" I ask her.

"Yes!" she snaps. "It was my cat, Fluffy!"

"Sorry!" I say.

"I shooed the dog off," she tells us.

We go past an angry man.

He points to the ground.

"Look at that!" he yells. So we do.

Oh no, big paw prints!

"I bet that's Buster," Lewis says.

"Shushhh!" we all tell him.

And we move on – quickly!

"Hey! Look over there!" Harvey yells.

Buster!

He is by the swings.

A little girl and her mum are patting him.

"Buster!" I shout.

He turns and wags his tail.

We all run over to the swings.

But as we do, Buster grabs the little girl's ice cream, and then he's off again!

The little girl is crying. Her mum is angry.

Ravi hands her some coins.

"Sorry! Here you go!" he says. "Buy a new one!"

We hurry on after Buster.

Buster is too fast for us.

We lose him again, but then we hear a dog bark.

"That sounds like Buster!" I yell.

The dog is behind a fence, and it is too high to see over.

I stand on Harvey to look.

"Is it Buster?" they all ask.

"Er, no…" I say.

We hurry on and turn out of Smith Way, past the old swimming pool.

"Hey! Over there!" yells Ravi.

We all look.

It's Buster! He is sniffing around some bins.

We all run over.

"Here, Buster!" I yell. "Here, boy!"

Buster turns around.

He wags his tail. Then he runs off again around the next corner.

Buster thinks this is a game!

Chapter Four

"Buster is never gonna let us catch him!" I groan.

"What are you gonna do now?" Lewis asks.

The crew all look worried for me.

I hang my head.

"I'm gonna have to see Calvin, guys," I say.

"We'll come with you," says Harvey.

"That's what the crew is for," says Amber.

So we all head over to Calvin's place.

"Wish me luck, guys," I say, as we turn the corner.

I look over at Calvin's front door.

My heart is thumping and then I see a big hairy lump on the mat outside.

It can't be. Can it?

Buster?

IT IS!

Buster is outside Calvin's door.

He is fast asleep.

We all creep over there.

"Shhh…" I say. "Don't wake him – or he'll run off again."

I bend down and pick up Buster's lead.

Result!

Buster wakes up with a loud snort.

He sees me and wags his tail.

And then I feel a BIG hand on my arm.

It's Calvin!

"Nice one, Sam," Calvin says.

Phew! We were just in time.

Calvin hands me ten pounds. "Here you go, Sam."

"Er…thanks," I say.

I put the money in my pocket.

"Was Buster good?" Calvin asks me.

I hand him Buster's lead.

"Yeah…no trouble at all," I lie.

Calvin looks at Buster, then he looks at me and shrugs. "Sweet," he says.

"Coz most of the time, he just runs off home!"

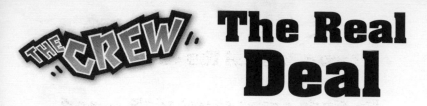

The Real Deal

I'm walking home from my nan's,
past the old swimming pool.

It's been closed for a long time.

There are boards across the doors.

I want to have a look in there.

So I push a loose board to one side,
and I go in.

It's really dark, so I turn on my mobile
to see.

I'm in a big, dusty room.

The dust makes me sneeze!

There are loads of boxes on the floor.

The boxes are full of stuff – iPods,
mobiles, laptops.

Boy… where has it all come from?

And why is it here?

I bet it's stolen.

Lewis is in at the deep end!

He finds some great stuff — and lots of cash — hidden at the old swimming pool. It must be stolen, and that spells trouble!

13 July.

Catch up with all THE CREW adventures!

978 0 7496 9038 0

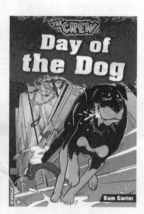

978 0 7496 9039 7

978 0 7496 9042 7

978 0 7496 9041 0

978 0 7496 9040 3

978 0 7496 9037 3